Yohance and the Dinosaurs

Alexis Obi

For Dawne and Sarah

YYOHANCE AND THE DINOSAURS
TAMARIND BOOKS 9781870516341

Published in Great Britain by Tamarind Books,
a division of Random House Children's Books
A Random House Group Company

This edition published 1996
Reprinted 2008

1 3 5 7 9 10 8 6 4 2

TAMARIND BOOKS
61–63 Uxbridge Road, London, W5 5SA

www.**tamarindbooks**.co.uk
www.**kids**at**randomhouse**.co.uk

Addresses for companies within The Random House Group Limited can be found at:
www.randomhouse.co.uk/offices.htm

THE RANDOM HOUSE GROUP Limited Reg. No. 954009

A CIP catalogue record for this book is available from the British Library.

Printed and bound in Singapore

Yohance and the Dinosaurs

Alexis Obi

Illustrated by Lynne Willey

Tamarind

Yohance loved dinosaurs.
He read about them
and wrote about them.
He asked for them at Christmas
and he saw them in the clouds.

Early morning
was a good time.
Yohance would tiptoe
onto the veranda
to watch the sunrise,
the dinosaurs
and the lizards.

Once, when he watched
the fishermen get ready
for work, he asked them.
'Have you ever seen
enormous sea creatures
far, far out
near where the sea
meets the sky?'

'No, oh no! Never,'
they replied.

'Have you seen dinosaurs in the sky?'
asked Yohance.
'No, oh no! Never!' they replied.
'I have,' said Yohance.
'I see dinosaurs in the sky.
Always.'

One day, he stopped
to talk to some picnickers.

'Have you seen dinosaurs in the sky?'
he asked.
'No, oh no! Never,' they replied.
'I have,' said Yohance.
'Always.'

The woman in the green cap said,
'That boy has his head
in the clouds.'

'Is my head in the clouds?'
Yohance asked his mother.
'No, you have a good imagination.
Let's go for a walk.'

They walked
among the trees,
along the beach
and right across the bay.

Here, stormy, sun stealing
dinosaurs gathered.
Here, the sea rolled itself
into huge waves
and rushed to the shore,
fussing and hissing and foaming.

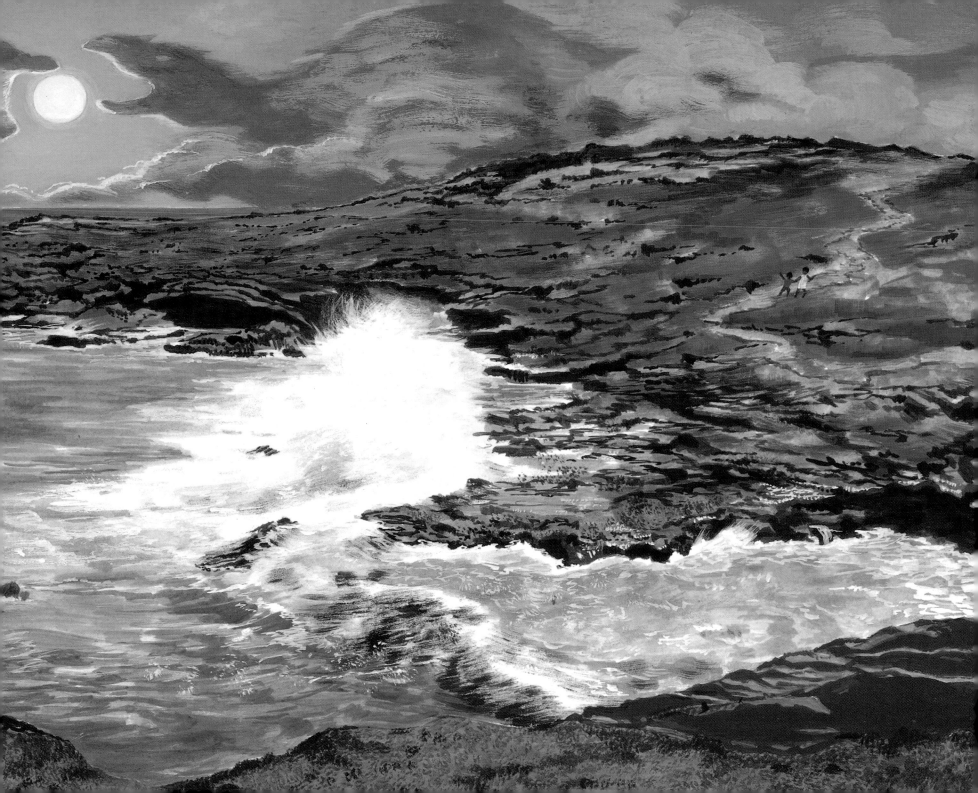

Mother took his hand
and hurried back home
to hide from the rain.

In his room
he sat quietly and read
all about his favourite creatures.

Outside, loud thunder pounded
like Tyrannosaurus
and Apatosaurus
and Stegosaurus at war.

Yohance's mother made him
a fantastic costume.
He pretended to be
the fiercest dinosaur ever.

At the carnival
he won a prize.

At rehearsal
for the school play,
it was time
to have fun in the Ark,
for chickens
even for silly mice
and rabbits.

It was not the right time
for dinosaurs.

Sunset was a good time.
Some dinosaurs wore their
best colours.
Scarlet tinged with blue and
purple tinged with orange.

One evening, as Yohance watched,
some sun stealing dinosaurs
floated across the skies.
'Don't swallow the sun!' he yelled.
They stopped.
The sun escaped
and slipped a little closer to the sea.

The mighty dinosaurs then
glared at each other.
Others gathered.
The leader took the
shape of the lizard
which sat by his window.

Then she grew to look
like the iguana
his father brought home
from the mountain.

'Get back Iguanadon!'
yelled Yohance.
Mother hurried out to the veranda.
'What's all this shouting about?
Don't get over excited.
It's nearly bedtime.'

But Yohance wasn't tired.
Not even one little bit.
He waved his arms,
his imagination took off
and Triceratops gave him a ride.

Yohance and Triceratops
joined Apatosaurus.
They joined forces with the wind,
jostling and pushing and shoving,
in a mighty battle to save the sun.

Yohance and his friends
scattered the sun stealers
and blew them back across the bay.

The sun went peacefully to rest
before she rose again
in the morning.

Yohance flew back to his room,
jumped into his pyjamas
and dived under the mosquito net.

Just then, mother came in
to read him a bedtime story.

Soon, soft darkness fell
and Yohance dreamed about
dinosaurs, as usual.

Other Tamarind titles available:

FOR READERS OF YOHANCE AND THE DINOSAURS

The Dragon Kite
Mum's Late
Marty Monster
The Bush
The Feather
Princess Katrina and the Hair Charmer
Boots for a Bridesmaid
Starlight

BOOKS FOR WHEN YOU GET A LITTLE OLDER...
The Day Ravi Smiled
Ferris Fleet the Wheelchair Wizard
Hurricane

NON-FICTION

BLACK STARS BIOGRAPHY
Rudolph Walker – Actor
Benjamin Zephaniah – Poet
Malorie Blackman – Author
Samantha Tross – Surgeon
Baroness Scotland of Asthal – Queen's Counsel and Politician
Jim Brathwaite – Entrepreneur
Lord Taylor of Warwick – Barrister
Chinwe Roy – Artist

The Life of Stephen Lawrence
The History of the Steel Band

and if you are interested in seeing the rest of our list, please visit our website:
www.**tamarindbooks**.co.uk